DESTINY
THE GRAPHIC NOVEL

CREATED BY

MICHAEL GLOVER & D.V. NOBLES

DESTINY -THE GRAPHIC NOVEL, EPISODE #1, "FINALE" Published by DVNobles Publishing.
Copyright © 2017 By D.V. Nobles - All rights reserved.
Story, concept and design, all artwork, models, layout and final production created by Michael Glover and D.V. Nobles. Destiny and the Destiny universe, including but not limited to, characters, ship designs, set designs, device and technology concepts, story and story concepts are the sole creation and property of the co-creators. This is a work of science-fiction and any similarity to persons living or dead or to other fictional works is purely coincidental. Any reproduction of this work or the use of Destiny concepts or designs in whole or in part are by permission only. The creators of Destiny wish to acknowledge theBlender Foundation (www.blender.org), MakeHuman (www.makehuman.org), Adobe (www.adobe.com), Digital Anarchy (www.digitalanarchy.com), and www.textures.com.

Michael Glover wishes to thank his mother, Dale Glover,
Michelle Clark and his daughter, Halie.
D.V. Nobles wishes to thank his wife, Susan.

Dedicated to those who still believe in the future...

PROLOGUE

IN THE FUTURE, THE CONQUEST OF SPACE IS DOMINATED BY CORPORATIONS DETERMINED TO OBTAIN RESOURCES FROM THE OUTER REACHES TO FEED THEIR BOTTOM LINE.

COMPETITION FOR OWNERSHIP AND MINING OF CERTAIN OUTPOSTS IS FIERCE AND A CORPORATE WAR BREAKS OUT BETWEEN THE TWO LEADING BUSINESS FACTIONS.

EVENTUALLY, A TREATY IS REACHED AND THE OPPOSING CORPORATIONS MERGE TO FORM THE LARGEST CONGLOMERATE EVER TO EXIST, *THE EARTH SPACE CONSORTIUM (ESC)*. ON ITS FACE, THE *ESC* CLAIMS ITS PRIMARY MISSION IS FOR THE BETTERMENT OF HUMANKIND, BUT MANY BELIEVE IT IS JUST ANOTHER FRONT FOR CORPORATE DOMINATION AND GREED.

EVEN SO, THE HUMAN RACE IS ON THE VERGE OF BECOMING A TRUE SPACE-FARING CIVILIZATION. THERE ARE STILL THOSE WHO BELIEVE THAT SPACE EXPLORATION AND THE DISCOVERIES THAT IT HOLDS FAR OUTWEIGH THE BLIND QUEST TO EXPLOIT MATERIAL RESOURCES.

THIS IS THE STORY OF THE *ESC DESTINY* AND HER CREW...

25 YEARS AGO, THE ESC DESTINY WAS LOST IN A SPACIAL ANOMALY ACCIDENT. HER CAPTAIN, CHARLES MASSEY, NEVER GAVE UP THE SEARCH FOR HIS SHIP.

TWO WEEKS AGO, WITHOUT WARNING, THE DESTINY'S NAVIGATIONAL BEACON CAME ONLINE.

CAPTAIN MASSEY ENLISTED THE HELP OF HIS FRIEND AND FORMER SECOND-IN-COMMAND, COMMANDER JACKSON.

TOGETHER, THEY EMBARKED ON A ONE-WAY TRIP IN HOPES OF FINDING THEIR LOST SHIP. AND TO DISCOVER THE TRUTH ABOUT WHAT HAPPENED

...ALL THOSE YEARS AGO.

EPISODE 1: "FINALE"

I CAN'T BELIEVE IT, JAX. IT'S REALLY HER...

JAX, CAN YOU MATCH HER ROTATION?

WORKING ON IT NOW, CAPTAIN.

SLOWLY, EXPERTLY, DR. JACKSON MATCHES THE SHUTTLE'S ROTATION WITH THE *DESTINY*...

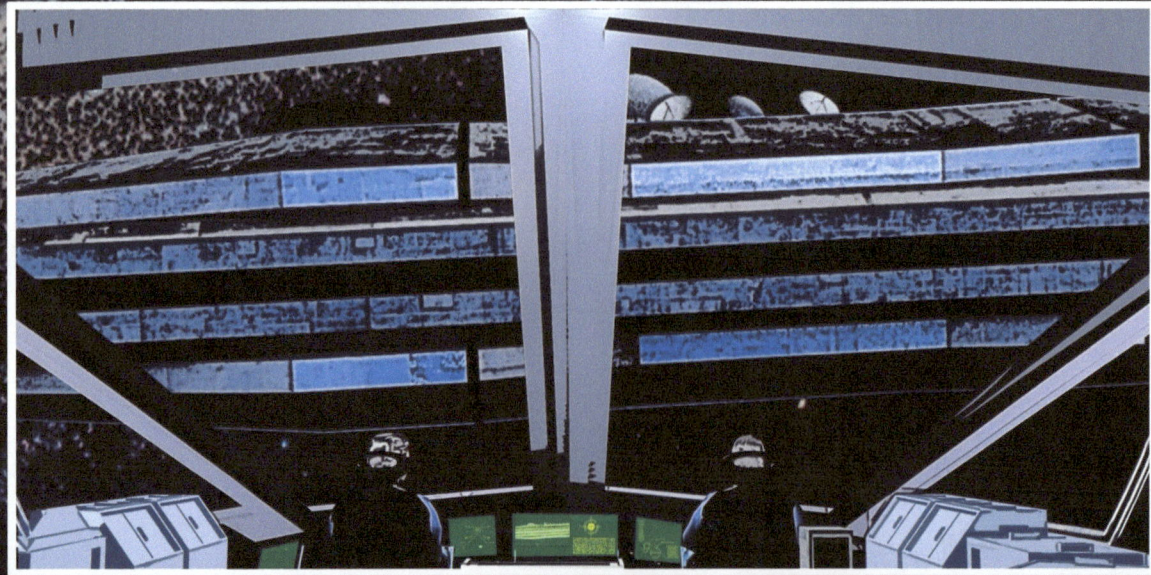

ON BOARD THE DERELICT DESTINY....

JAX, CHECK OUT ENGINEERING. SEE IF YOU CAN GET THE EMERGENCY POWER UP.

AYE, CAPTAIN. WHERE ARE YOU HEADED?

THE BRIDGE.

MY SHIP... LOST FOR THE LAST 25 YEARS... SO MANY MEMORIES WERE HERE... NOW JUST DARK CORRIDORS.

CAPTAIN, THE MAIN DOORS TO ENGINEERING ARE ON EMERGENCY LOCKDOWN, AS I SUSPECTED....IT'S GOING TO TAKE SOME TIME TO GET ONE OPEN.

TAKE YOUR TIME, JAX. WE HAVE — WHAT— 2 HOURS WORTH OF AIR?

DON'T REMIND ME.... THIS COULD BE OUR FINAL RESTING PLACE. I GUESS WE COULD ALWAYS GET BACK IN THE SHUTTLE WITH WHAT LITTLE FUEL WE HAVE AND PRAY SOMEONE HEARS OUR DISTRESS CALL....

NO....

SIR, IF I MAY... NOT TO DOUBT COMMANDER JACKSON'S ACHIEVEMENTS — AFTER ALL, THE HYPER GRAVITATIONAL TECH-NOLOGY HE PIONEERED IS THE REASON LONG-RANGE SPACE TRAVEL IS WHAT IT IS TODAY — BUT WE ARE TALKING ABOUT HARNESSING AN ENERGY THAT, QUITE FRANKLY, I DON'T THINK WE ARE READY FOR.

NOTED, MISS ARROWAY... AND I WILL ADD THERE WAS SOME HESITATION FROM THE COUNCIL AS WELL. CAPTAIN MASSEY, I'M SURE YOU UNDER-STAND YOU MUST TAKE *FULL* RESPONSIBILITY OF THE OVERALL SAFETY OF THIS EXPERIMENT...

OF COURSE, SIR.

THEN GOOD LUCK TO YOU AND YOUR CREW. I LOOK FOR-WARD TO POSITIVE RESULTS NEXT WEEK...STINSON OUT.

WELL, JAX. I THINK THIS CALLS FOR A BIT OF A CELE-BRATION. WANT TO TELL YOUR TEAM THE GOOD NEWS?

YES, SIR! AND...THANKS FOR THE VOTE OF CONFIDENCE, MISS ARROWAY...

I DON'T THINK HE UNDERSTOOD. I DIDN'T MEAN TO QUESTION HIS ABILITIES...

HE'LL GET OVER IT.

CAPTAIN CHARLES MASSEY — AGE 31 AT ESC DESTINY LAUNCH TIME

2.241 — JOINED **EARTH-SPACE CONSORTIUM (ESC)** AT AGE 19 IN SEARCH OF A CAREER IN PILOTING AND NAVIGATION

2242 — SERVED ABOARD THE **ESC FORD**, A MINING FREIGHTER, FOR 2 YEARS

2244 — ASSIGNED TO THE **ESC KAMEN** WHERE COMMANDER LOUIS KEVLER TOOK HIM UNDER HIS WING, OFTEN ALLOWING HIM TO COMMAND THE VESSEL AND PERFORM MANEUVERS NOT SANCTIONED BY THE **ESC**. DURING THIS TIME, MASSEY REALIZED HIS LOVE FOR SPACE EXPLORATION AND GREW WEARY OF THE **ESC'S** CONSTANT DEMANDS ON PRODUCTION DEADLINES.

IN 2248, AN ACCIDENTAL EXPLOSION CRIPPLED THE **ESC KAMEN** AND TOOK THE LIVES OF 12 CREWMEMBERS, INCLUDING COMMANDER KEVLER. MASSEY WAS COMMENDED FOR SECURING THE SAFETY OF THE REMAINING CREW AND SUCCESSFULLY DELIVERING THE SHIP'S EXPENSIVE PAYLOAD.

2249 — PLANNED TO LEAVE THE **ESC** AND BECOME AN INDEPENDENT CAPTAIN WHEN APPROACHED BY HIS FRIEND, DR. SIMON "JAX" JACKSON. DR. JACKSON CONVINCED MASSEY TO USE HIS NEWFOUND HERO STATUS TO HELP HIM APPROACH THE **ESC** WITH A REQUEST TO CREATE THE MOST ADVANCED VESSEL OF EXPLORATION EVER CONCEIVED. THE VESSEL, THE **ESC DESTINY**, WOULD BE THE FIRST PRODUCTION SHIP TO IMPLEMENT DR. JACKSON'S HYPER-GRAVITATIONAL PROPULSION TECHNOLOGY. THE **ESC** AGREED, BUT THEY DEMANDED MAJORITY RIGHTS TO THE TECHNOLOGY. THE ESC ALSO DICTATED THAT THE SHIP WOULD BE USED TO CLAIM RESOURCES AND THAT MASSEY WOULD AGREE TO A TEN YEAR CONTRACT AS CONTINUING EMPLOYEE WITH THE **ESC**.

2253 — THE **ESC DESTINY** IS LAUNCHED WITH CHARLES MASSEY AS CAPTAIN.

==QECOM ENCRYPTED MESSAGE==

SINGULARITY DRIVE EQUATIONS SECURED.

EXCELLENT! SEND THEM THROUGH THIS SECURED CHANNEL.

NO. I WILL DELIVER THEM IN PERSON WHEN I GET MY PAYMENT.... AS PER OUR AGREEMENT.

VERY WELL. HOWEVER, I REMIND YOU THAT IF THE ESC CONTINUES TO POSSESS THE EQUATIONS, THEN THEY ARE OF MUCH LESSOR VALUE TO US. HOW DO YOU PROPOSE TO REMOVE THEM FROM EVERY POSSIBLE QUANTUM STORAGE DEVICE THAT MAY CONTAIN THEM?

LEAVE THAT TO ME.

<<ENCRYPT

SHIP'S ARBORETUM....

I'M GOING TO TURN IN FOR THE EVENING. IS THERE ANY—THING ELSE YOU NEED FROM ME?

NO, CAMERON. I'M GOING TO GET SOME REST MYSELF. TOMORROW'S GOING TO BE A BIG DAY.

I CAN'T BELIEVE THEY'RE STILL GOING THROUGH WITH THIS! I THOUGHT YOU WERE GOING TO WARN THE COUNCIL ABOUT THE DANGERS...

I VOICED MY CONCERN. IT WAS NOTED. MAKE NO MISTAKE, CAMERON...I AM FULLY AWARE OF THE INHERENT DANGERS. BUT THE BENEFITS WOULD BE FAR GREATER. BESIDES, EXPLORING THE UNKNOWN IS WHAT THIS SHIP'S ALL ABOUT.

YOU'VE CHANGED SO MUCH OVER THE TIME WE'VE BEEN ON THIS BLOODY SHIP. IT'S ALMOST LIKE YOU'VE FORGOTTEN THE REASON THE *ESC* SENT US HERE...

I KNOW WHY *I'M* HERE. THE QUESTION IS... WHY ARE *YOU* STILL HERE? I ORDERED YOU A RETURN SHUTTLE OVER A MONTH AGO!

YES, STRANGE. IT SEEMS IT'S BEEN...DELAYED.

DR. SIMON "JAX" JACKSON — AGE 31 AT ESC DESTINY LAUNCH TIME

2239 — ENTERED ORION INSTITUTE OF AERONAUTICS AT AGE 17 TO PURSUE A DEGREE IN ASTROPHYSICS.

2242 — EARNED DOCTORATE IN ASTROPHYSICS AND WAS IMMEDIATELY RECRUITED INTO PROJECT ANDROMEDA, A COLLABORATION OF SCIENTISTS WORKING TOWARDS ADVANCED SPACECRAFT PROPULSION SYSTEMS.

2246 — INDIVIDUALLY MADE A MAJOR BREAKTHROUGH IN THEORETICAL PROPULSION WHICH HE CALLED HYPER-GRAVITATIONAL PROPULSION. AFTER PRESENTING HIS THEORIES TO PROJECT ANDROMEDA, HE WAS GIVEN HIS OWN TEAM AND MADE PROJECT LEAD IN ORDER TO DEVELOP THE THEORETICAL PROPULSION SYSTEM.

2247 — SUFFERED A MAJOR BREAKDOWN DUE TO LACK OF SLEEP AND STRESS OF LEADING HIS TEAM.

2248 — SUCCESSFULLY CONDUCTED THREE SEPARATE TESTS OF THE HYPER-GRAVITATIONAL PROPULSION SYSTEM ON TEST VESSELS.

2249 — AFTER THE DISBANDMENT OF PROJECT ANDROMEDA, DR. JACKSON BEGAN SEARCHING FOR A BENEFACTOR TO IMPLEMENT HIS NEW PROPULSION TECHNOLOGY ON A LARGE-SCALE PRODUCTION VESSEL. BELIEVING THE *ESC* WOULD BE THE ONLY CORPORATE ENTITY POWERFUL ENOUGH TO DO THIS, HE SOUGHT OUT HIS FRIEND, CHARLES MASSEY, TO HELP HIM APPROACH THE *ESC*.

2253 — *ESC DESTINY* LAUNCHED AS THE FIRST PRODUCTION VESSEL TO INCORPORATE THE NEW HYPER-GRAVITATIONAL PROPULSION SYSTEM. DR. JACKSON, NOW EMPLOYED BY THE *ESC*, WAS RELUCTANTLY BROUGHT ABOARD AS SECOND-IN-COMMAND WITH DIRECTIVES TO MONITOR AND FURTHER ENHANCE THE TECHNOLOGY.

2258 — AFTER FURTHER BREAKTHROUGHS BY SCIENTISTS BACK ON EARTH, DR. JACKSON REALIZES HIS PROPULSION TECHNOLOGY CAN BE FURTHER ADVANCED AND THEORIZES THE SINGULARITY DRIVE.

2259 — WITH APPROVAL FROM THE *ESC*, DR. JACKSON PREPARES TO TEST HIS NEW PROPULSION SYSTEM ABOARD THE *ESC DESTINY*.

JAX... I CAN'T JUST... LEAVE HER...

CAPTAIN, WE'VE DONE ALL WE CAN... IT'S TIME TO GO.

CAPTAIN, I'M GETTING REPORTS THAT MEDLAB IS NEARLY AT CAPACITY. LIFEPODS ARE BEING OCCUPIED AND JETTISONED!

GOOD! WE'LL TAKE ONE OF THE SHUTTLES, BUT THERE ARE ONLY THREE CYRO CHAMBERS. LT. NORTH, GET TO THE MEDLAB IMMEDIATELY!

AYE, CAPTAIN. SEE YOU ON THE OTHER SIDE!

ABOARD THE SHUTTLE, *ESC KAKU*...

JAX, GET US OUT OF HERE! CAPTAIN MASSEY TO MEDLAB- DOCTOR DETRICK, REPORT-

AT CAPACITY, CAPTAIN- I'M NOT READING ANYONE ELSE ON THE SHIP, EXCEPT THOSE IN LIFEPODS- WE'RE JETTISONING THE MEDLAB *NOW!*

AS THE DESTINY IS PULLED EVER CLOSER TO CERTAIN DOOM, THE MEDLAB, NOW SERVING AS A LIFEBOAT FOR MUCH OF THE CREW, BREAKS FREE...

IN A DESPERATE ATTEMPT TO ESCAPE THE RIFT, HUNDREDS OF LIFEPODS JETTISON FROM THE DESTINY ALONG WITH THE MEDLAB AND THE THREE ON-BOARD SHUTTLES...

THE **DESTINY** IS PULLED HELPLESSLY TOWARDS THE RIFT...

FOR A FEW BRIEF SECONDS AN OPENING APPEARS...

AND THEN...

NOTHING.

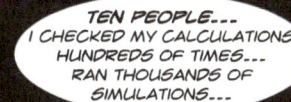

JAX, THIS IS *MY* RESPONSIBILITY, NOT YOURS. WE WILL FIGURE IT OUT AND FIND THE *DESTINY* IF SHE'S STILL OUT THERE SOMEWHERE. IN THE MEANTIME, I WANT THE TWO OF YOU TO GET INTO CRYRO. IT WILL BE A FEW MONTHS BEFORE ANY RESCUE SHIPS CAN GET TO US THIS FAR OUT...

AND YOU, CAPTAIN?

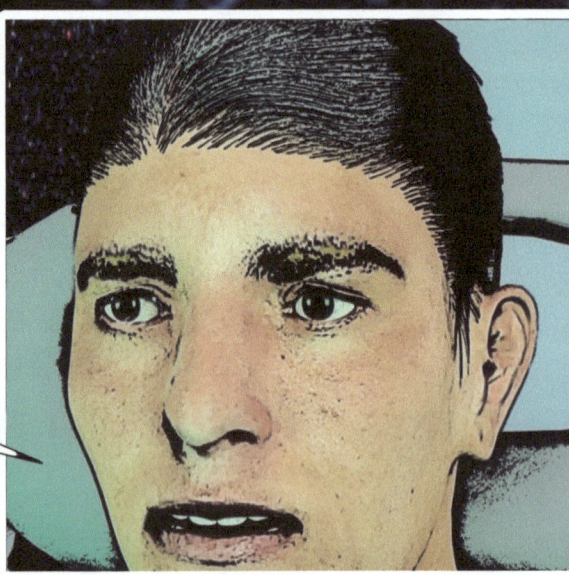

I NEED TO SEND A QECCOM TO THE *ESC* TO LET THEM KNOW OUR STATUS... AND I NEED TO CONFIRM THAT OUR REMAINING CREW ARE PUT TO SLEEP. I'LL BE RIGHT BEHIND YOU.

THREE WEEKS LATER...

MISS AMELIA ARROWAY – AGE 27 AT ESC DESTINY LAUNCH TIME

2246 – 2253 – EARNED MULTIPLE DEGREES AND ACCREDITATIONS.

2254 – JOINED THE **ESC** AS HEAD OF THE DIVISION OF ACQUISITIONS. SUBSEQUENTLY FIRED MOST OF THE DIVISION AND REPLACED THEM WITH FEWER PEOPLE.

2255 – WAS SINGLE-HANDEDLY RESPONSIBLE FOR A LARGE REDUCTION IN MINING PERSONNEL AND IMPLEMENTED CHANGES THAT RESULTED IN A STEEP RISE IN NET PROFIT RESULTS.

2256 – CAME ABOARD **ESC DESTINY** AS A "LIAISON" WITH THE **ESC**, HAVING STRICT ORDERS TO INVESTIGATE THE CREW AND TO ENSURE **ESC** INTERESTS ARE BEING LOOKED AFTER.

YES SIR, BUT AS I MENTIONED—

—AND DR. JACKSON, IT HAS COME TO OUR ATTENTION THAT YOU HAVE A POSSIBLE SUB-STANCE ABUSE PROBLEM?

SIR, I—

—DR. JACKSON, YOU ARE TO TURN OVER TO THE ESC ALL THE MATERIAL IN YOUR POSSESSION ON THE SINGULARITY DRIVE EXPERIMENT INCLUDING ALL EQUATIONS, THEORIES AND TEST RESULTS THEREOF.

COMMANDER JACKSON HAS BEEN WORKING ON THIS FOR YEARS! THIS TECHNOLOGY....IF IT WERE TO FALL INTO THE WRONG HANDS...

IT WOULD SEEM IT WAS ALREADY IN THE WRONG HANDS.

I AM COMPLETELY APPALLED BY THE ACTIONS OF THIS COUNCIL! THERE IS NO WAY YOU CAN KNOW THE ACHIEVEMENTS OF THESE MEN AND THE CREW OF THE **DESTINY** WITHOUT HAVING BEEN THERE. WHAT HAPPENED WAS A TRAGEDY, THERE IS NO QUESTION. BUT TO BLINDLY PASS JUDGEMENT ON THESE MEN IS WRONG! IF YOU READ MY REPORT YOU WOULD SEE THAT!

WE **HAVE** READ YOUR REPORT, MISS ARROWAY. WE HAVE ALSO REVIEWED ALL YOUR PAST RE-PORTS SINCE BEING ASSIGNED AS LIASON TO THE **ESC DESTINY**. IN THEM, WE COULD SEE A CAPTAIN WHO CLEARLY HAD INTERESTS OTHER THAN THOSE OF THE **ESC** IN MIND, EVEN GOING ON SOME PERSONAL VENDETTA MISSION. WE LEARNED OF A SECOND-IN-COMMAND THAT NOT ONLY HAD POSSIBLE SUBSTANCE ABUSE PROB-LEMS, BUT WAS UNABLE TO PERSONALLY COPE WITH THE RUN-IN HE HAD WITH THE ALLIANCE AND WAS UNFIT TO PERFORM COMMAND DUTIES IN THE CAPTAIN'S ABSENSE. WE ALSO LEARNED THAT THE SHIP'S NAVIGATOR WAS ORIGINALLY A DRUG-RUNNER WITH A DEEP HATRED OF THE **ESC** AND WAS ALLOWED TO WORK ON THE BRIDGE DOING ONE OF THE MOST CRUCIAL JOBS ON THE SHIP! SHALL I GO ON, MISS ARROWAY?

YOU ARE TAKING MY REPORTS OUT OF CONTEXT. AS MY MANAGER WILL ATTEST, I —

SIGH...YOU NO LONGER REPORT TO YOUR PREVIOUS MANAGER, MISS ARROWAY. YOU WILL BE REASSIGNED TO A DIFFERENT SECTION.

NO, SIR. I WILL NOT.

EXCUSE ME?

I RESIGN.

ZZZZ

BEEEEEP...

BEEEEEP...

BEEEEEP...

BEEEEEP...

JAX...
GET OVER
HERE...
NOW!

BEEEEEP...

KAYLA NORTH — AGE 30 AT ESC DESTINY LAUNCH TIME

2241 — FOUND HER WAY ABOARD MANY DIFFERENT SUPPLY SHIPS TO HONE HER PILOTING SKILLS.

2242 — ATTEMPTED TO GET AN OFFICIAL JOB AS AN APPRENTICE PILOT BY JOINING THE **ESC**. ONE WEEK LATER SHE WAS FIRED FOR INSUBORDINATION AND INAPPROPRIATE CONDUCT.

2244 — INHERITED HER FIRST SHIP, THE **RUST BUCKET**, FROM HER GRANDFATHER.

2245 — ARRESTED FOR TRANSPORTING ILLEGAL SUPPLIES AND PASSENGERS.

2246 — ARRESTED THREE TIMES IN THE SAME YEAR FOR TRANSPORTING ILLEGAL SUPPLIES AS WELL AS LACK OF PROPER VESSEL REGISTRATION.

2247 — FLEW THE **RUST BUCKET** INTO AN **ESC** SUPPLY CENTER AND PURPOSELY DESTROYED MOST OF THE FACILITY. SHE WAS SUBSEQUENTLY ARRESTED, HER SHIP PERMANENTLY IMPOUNDED AND PILOTING LICENSE SUSPENDED INDEFINITELY.

2252 — WHILE HITCHING A RIDE ON A SUPPLY SHIP, SHE WAS ATTACKED BY THE PILOT. AFTER SHE SUBDUED HIM, SHE STRANDED HIM AT A MINING COLONY AND LEFT WITH HIS SHIP, THE **IRONSIDE**, WHICH SHE RENAMED THE **RUST BUCKET II**.

2256 — WAS RESCUED BY THE **ESC DESTINY** FROM AN ALLIANCE ATTACK ON HER SHIP. SOON AFTER COMING ABOARD, HER PILOTING SKILLS BECAME EVIDENT AND CAPTAIN MASSEY ATTEMPTED TO RECRUIT HER.

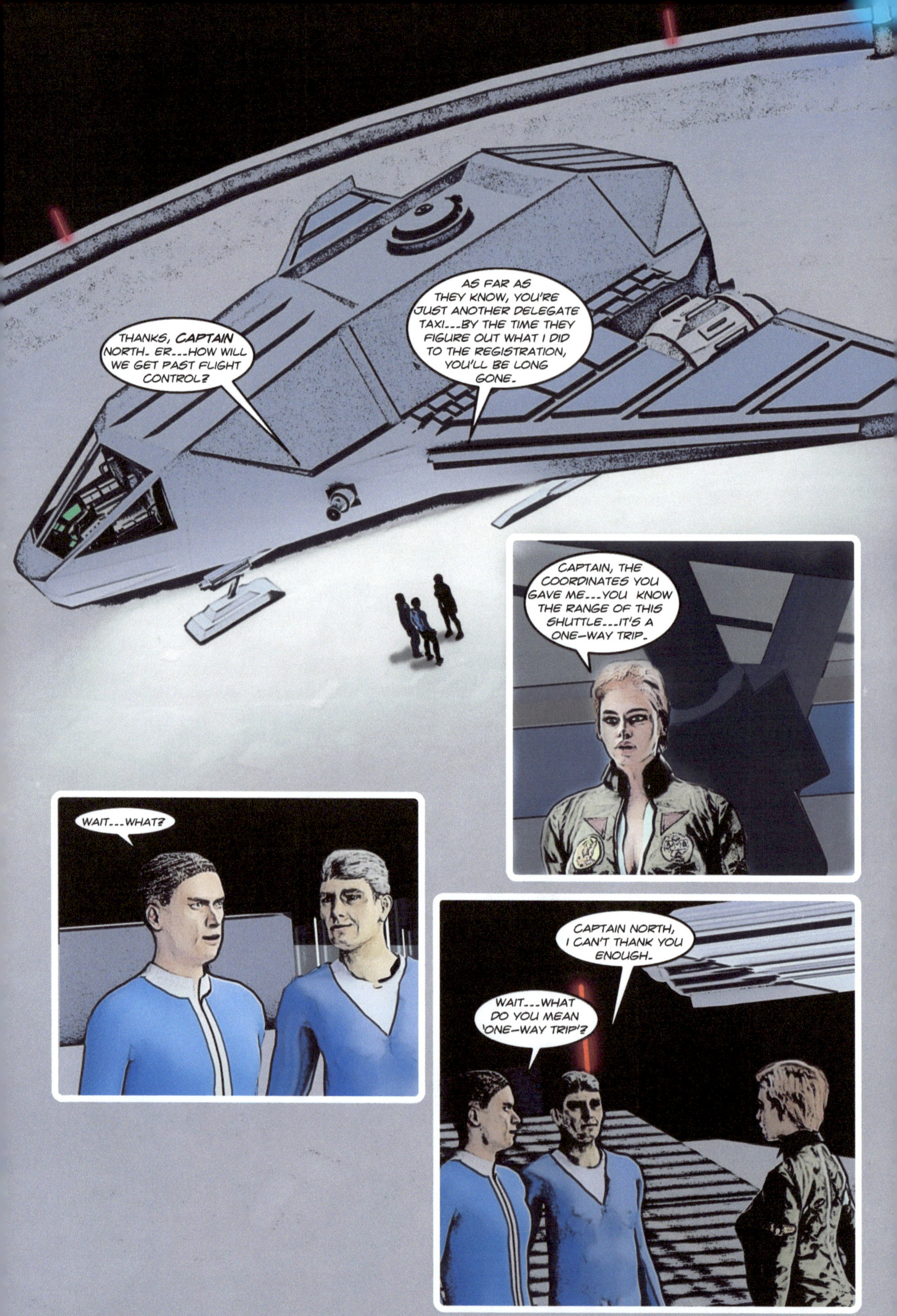

THANKS, *CAPTAIN* NORTH. ER...HOW WILL WE GET PAST FLIGHT CONTROL?

AS FAR AS THEY KNOW, YOU'RE JUST ANOTHER DELEGATE TAXI...BY THE TIME THEY FIGURE OUT WHAT I DID TO THE REGISTRATION, YOU'LL BE LONG GONE.

CAPTAIN, THE COORDINATES YOU GAVE ME...YOU KNOW THE RANGE OF THIS SHUTTLE...IT'S A ONE-WAY TRIP.

WAIT...WHAT?

CAPTAIN NORTH, I CAN'T THANK YOU ENOUGH.

WAIT...WHAT DO YOU MEAN 'ONE-WAY TRIP'?

DR. PETRICK   CMDR. "JAX" JACKSON   LT. NORTH   CAPTAIN MASSEY   CAMERON   MISS ARROWAY   LT. KADRA   CMDR. ZHANG

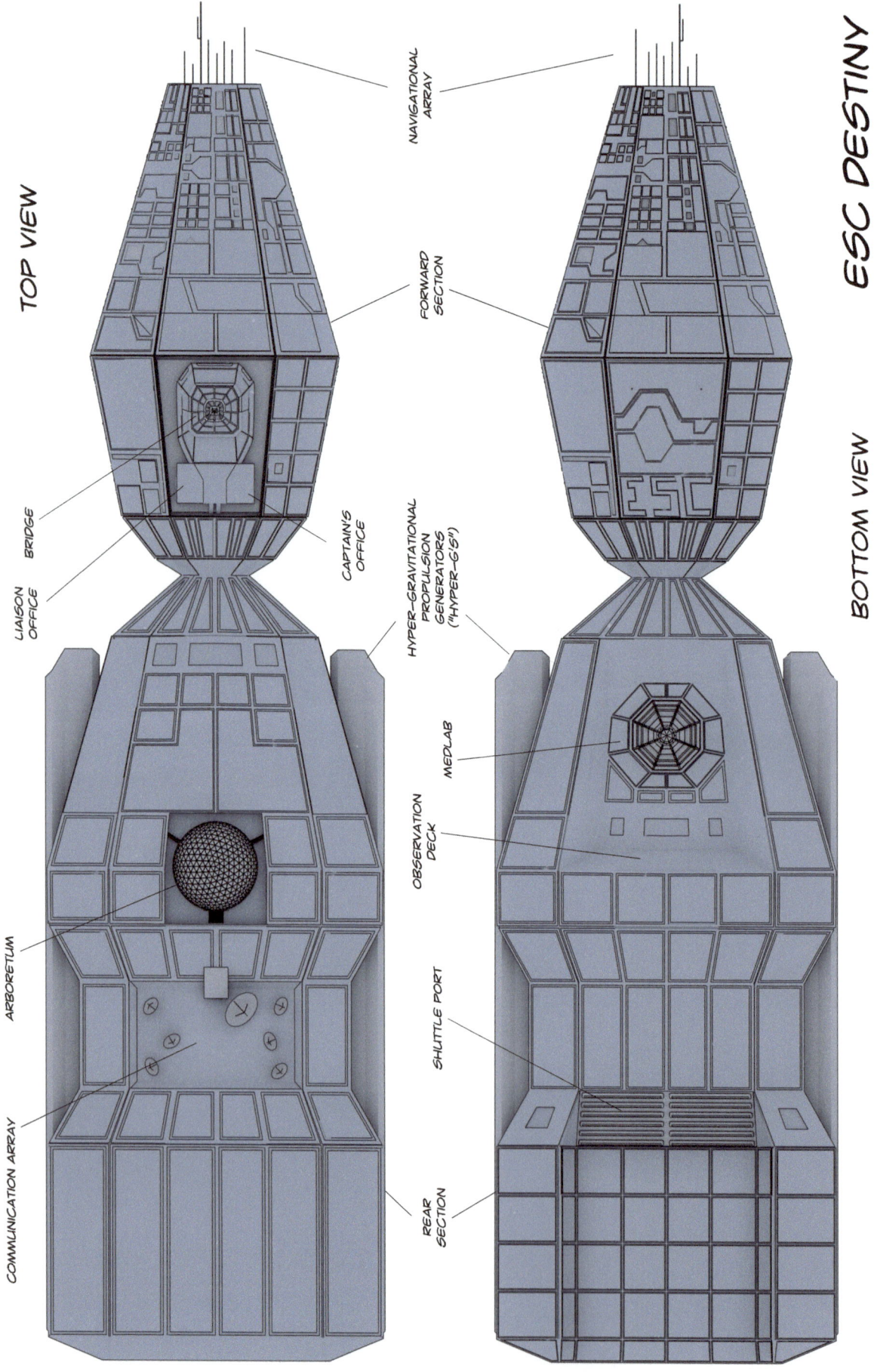

TOP VIEW

BOTTOM VIEW

ESC DESTINY

NAVIGATIONAL ARRAY

FORWARD SECTION

LIAISON OFFICE

BRIDGE

CAPTAIN'S OFFICE

HYPER-GRAVITATIONAL PROPULSION GENERATORS ("HYPER-G'S")

MEDLAB

ARBORETUM

OBSERVATION DECK

COMMUNICATION ARRAY

SHUTTLE PORT

REAR SECTION

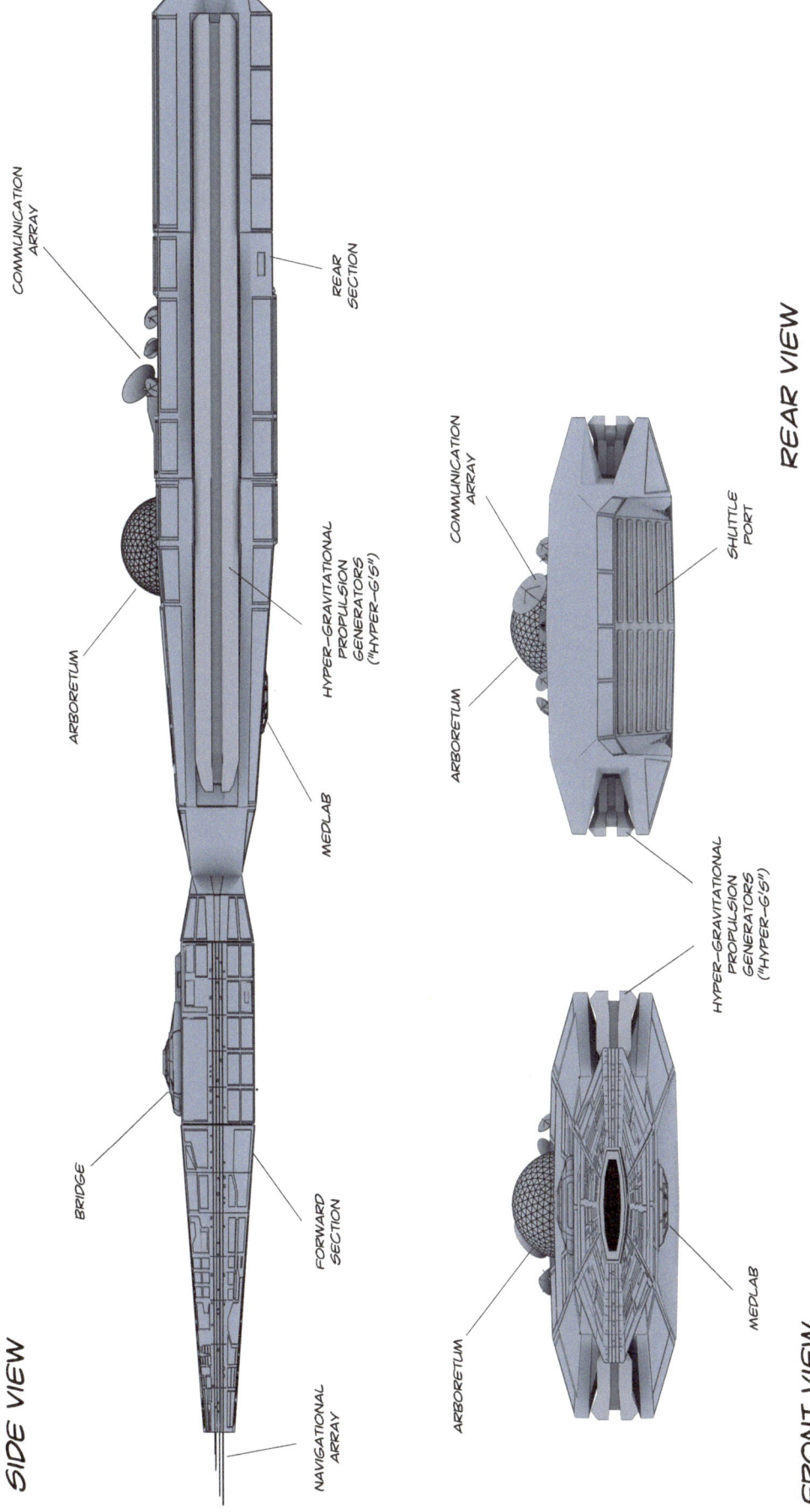

SIDE VIEW

COMMUNICATION ARRAY

REAR SECTION

ARBORETUM

HYPER-GRAVITATIONAL PROPULSION GENERATORS ("HYPER-G'S")

MEDLAB

BRIDGE

FORWARD SECTION

NAVIGATIONAL ARRAY

REAR VIEW

COMMUNICATION ARRAY

ARBORETUM

SHUTTLE PORT

HYPER-GRAVITATIONAL PROPULSION GENERATORS ("HYPER-G'S")

ARBORETUM

MEDLAB

FRONT VIEW

ESC DESTINY

DESTINY TIMELINE

2113
Most political factions and governments of the Earth are no more, given way to the rise of powerful corporations which govern and profit from every facet of society. Peace prevails, but inevitably some organizations grow hostile in order to feed their ever expanding bottom line.

2234
Two of the largest corporations on Earth clash in the pursuit of rights to mine claimed resources in space. A corporate war breaks out, with both sides breaking their own constitutions by preparing soldiers and weapons to fight each other.

2236
Realizing heavy profit and life loss on both sides, a treaty is finally reached. The two corporations merge, abandoning their previous names in order to form a single union, vowing never again to allow a fight for resources to escalate as it did. However, this union caused a mass exodus from both sides of those who fought against and hated their opposing corporation. Eventually, many of those who once fought each other came together to form their own alliance.

2237
The Earth Space Consortium (ESC) emerges as the world's largest corporate entity to exploit resources in space, often times under the guise of promoting space exploration.

2239
The group known as "The Alliance", and often referred to as 'pirates' begin raiding mining operations and attacking ESC ships and equipment.

2246
Dr. Simon Jackson leads a team of scientists to develop his theoretical Hyper-Gravitational Propulsion (Hyper-G) technology. Within three years, the technology is successful with an unexpected benefit - the ability to provide gravitational force on a ship with a large enough device.

2249
Dr. Jackson seeks out the help of his friend, Captain Charles Massey to approach the ESC with the technology. Captain Massey has long had dreams of commanding a ship that would be capable of going beyond the current boundaries of space exploration.. The ESC is the only corporation large enough to fund such a project, so they offer rights to Hyper-G technology in order to get the ship built. It is to be a vessel of exploration, but the ESC demands that it also be used to discover new mining resources.

2253
The ESC Destiny is completed and launches, commanded by Captain Charles Massey.. It is the largest exploration vessel ever built and the first to incorporate Hyper-G technology on a scale large enough to provide gravity aboard ship. Dr. Jackson comes on board as second-in-command, with the directive from the ESC to further enhance the Hyper-G propulsion system.

2258
With the success of the Hyper-G technology and recent breakthroughs by Astrophysicists on Earth, Dr. Jackson hypothesizes a completely new propulsion system called Singularity Drive, which theoretically would use a microscopic black hole to expand the Hyper-G propulsion. If successful, travel to very distant stars would be possible.

2259
The final phase of testing for the Singularity drive is implemented...

A MESSAGE FROM THE CREATORS...

TO SAY DESTINY IS SOMETHING THAT IS VERY CLOSE TO OUR HEARTS IS A MASSIVE UNDERSTATEMENT. FOR THE PAST 30 YEARS, WE HAVE BEEN HOPING, WISHING AND DREAMING THE DESTINY UNIVERSE INTO EXISTENCE, SEARCHING FOR A VIABLE WAY TO TELL THE DESTINY STORY. A WRITER IS FAMILIAR WITH THE FACT THAT CHARACTERS REALLY DO TAKE ON A LIFE OF THEIR OWN. THE DESTINY UNIVERSE AND ITS CHARACTERS HAS COME TO LIFE AND OFTEN WE FEEL LIKE WE ARE MERELY THE MEDIUM THEY ARE USING TO GET THEIR STORY TOLD. WHEN YOUR CHARACTERS START KICKING, SCREAM-ING AND PLEADING THEN YOU HAVE NO OTHER RECOURSE THAN TO DO THEIR BIDDING. OUR CHARACTERS HAVE BEEN PLEADING WITH US FOR A VERY, VERY LONG TIME TO BE BROUGHT OUT INTO THE OPEN AND ALLOWED TO EXIST IN SOMETHING MORE THAN JUST THE CONFINES OF OUR MINDS.

TO TRY TO APPEASE THESE VOICES IN OUR HEADS, WE MADE SEVERAL AT-TEMPTS OVER THE YEARS TO BRING DESTINY TO LIFE, WHETHER IT BE THROUGH WRITTEN NOTES, SHORT ANIMATIONS OR JUST DREAMING ABOUT DESTINY SCENES OVER A CUP OF COFFEE. EACH TIME WE TRIED, HOWEVER, THERE ALWAYS SEEMED TO BE SOME ROADBLOCK THAT TOLD US WE WEREN'T QUITE READY...IT JUST WASN'T THE RIGHT TIME. AT LONG LAST, THROUGH A MAGICAL SERIES OF EVENTS, THINGS FINALLY FELL INTO PLACE. THE DESTINY UNIVERSE BEGAN TO FORM MORE CLEARLY THAN EVER BEFORE. WE HAD THE TECHNOLOGY AVAILABLE TO US THAT DID NOT EXIST IN THE PAST AND THE NECESSARY EXPERIENCE TO USE IT TO TELL OUR STORY. THE CAST AND CREW OF DESTINY, FILLED WITH RELIEF AND WONDER AT WHAT THEIR FUTURE HELD, STEPPED BOLDLY FORWARD. THE WAIT WAS FINALLY OVER...

WE ARE TELLING THE DESTINY STORY BECAUSE WE FEEL IT'S A STORY THAT MUST BE TOLD. WE'VE INVESTED OUR HEARTS INTO THESE CHARACTERS AND AS THE STORY UNFOLDS, WE HOPE THAT SHINES THROUGH. JUST THE FACT THAT WE'VE FINALLY MADE IT THIS FAR FILLS US WITH HAPPINESS, BUT WE WANT TO BE ABLE TO TELL THE REST OF THE STORY. THAT'S WHERE YOU, THE SCI-FI FAN, COMES IN. WE CAN'T DO THIS ALONE AND NEED THE POWER OF OUR FELLOW SCI-FI FANS TO JOIN US FOR THE RIDE. IF YOU'VE ENJOYED THIS ISSUE AND WANT TO SEE MORE, PLEASE TELL OTHERS ABOUT DESTINY. REVIEWS ARE EXTREMELY IMPORTANT. PLEASE TAKE A MOMENT TO POST A REVIEW ON AMAZON. WE NEED GOOD REVIEWS TO BE SUCCESSFUL, BUT OF COURSE WE WANT YOU TO BE HONEST. IF YOU FOUND THIS WORK TO BE LESS THAN AT LEAST 3 STARS, PLEASE CONTACT US DIRECTLY AND LET US KNOW WHAT WE NEED TO DO TO IMPROVE.

THANK YOU AND KEEP ON LOOKING TO THE FUTURE...

D.V. NOBLES   MICHAEL GLOVER

WWW.DESTINYTGN.COM

www.ingramcontent.com/pod-product-compliance
Lightning Source LLC
Chambersburg PA
CBHW041000170626
46815CB00002B/83